FALKIRK COMMUNITY TRUST

30124 03108771 3

KU-750-418

Falkirk Community

Trust

30124 03108771 3	
Askews & Holts	
JF JF	£11.99
SL	

First published 2015 by Walker Books Ltd
87 Vauxhall Walk, London SE11 5HJ

2 4 6 8 10 9 7 5 3 1

© 2015 Lucy Cousins

The right of Lucy Cousins to be identified as author/illustrator of this
work has been asserted by her in accordance with the
Copyright, Designs and Patents Act 1988.

Maisy™. Maisy is a trademark of Walker Books Ltd, London.

This book has been typeset in Gill Sans MT Schoolbook and Lucy Cousins font.
Lucy Cousins font © 2015 Lucy Cousins.
Handlettering by Lucy Cousins.

Printed in China

All rights reserved. No part of this book may be reproduced,
transmitted or stored in an information retrieval system
in any form or by any means, graphic, electronic or mechanical,
including photocopying, taping and recording,
without prior written permission from the publisher.

British Library Cataloguing in Publication Data:
a catalogue record for this book is available from the British Library.

ISBN 978-1-4063-5731-8

www.walker.co.uk

Count with Maisy, Cheep, Cheep, Cheep!

Lucy Cousins

WALKER BOOKS
AND SUBSIDIARIES

LONDON · BOSTON · SYDNEY · AUCKLAND

It's nearly bedtime.
Mummy Hen is looking for her
10 chicks.

cluck,
cluck

CANCELLED

Maisy will help.

Are there any chicks in the stable?

cluck, cluck

Are there any chicks behind the gate?

Are there any chicks in the trailer?

Or in the tractor?

Are there any chicks in the apple tree?

Are there any chicks behind the lettuces?

Are there any chicks in the pigsty?

the flower-bed?

cluck, cluck

Is the last chick behind the sack,

or in the wheelbarrow,

quack qua

in the
beehive,

or behind the
watering can?

Is the last chick in the hay barn?

cluck, cluck, cluck, cluck,

Mummy Hen has found
all of her chicks!

Now it's bedtime.